Maiden of the Mist

A LEGEND OF NIAGARA FALLS

RETOLD AND ILLUSTRATED BY
VERONIKA MARTENOVA CHARLES

Fitzhenry & Whiteside

Text and illustrations copyright © 2001 by Veronika Martenova Charles

Published in Canada by Fitzhenry & Whiteside, 195 Allstate Parkway, Markham, Ontario, L3R 4T8

Published in the United States by Fitzhenry & Whiteside
311 Washington Street, Brighton, Massachusetts 02135

Fitzhenry & Whiteside acknowledges with thanks the Canada Council for the Arts, the Government of Canada through the Book Publishing Industry Development Program (BPIDP), and the Ontario Arts Council for their support for our publishing program.

www.fitzhenry.ca   godwit@fitzhenry.ca

Canadian Cataloguing in Publication Data

Charles, Veronika Martenova
Maiden of the mist

ISBN 0-7737-3297-7 (bound)   ISBN 0-7737-6207-8 (pbk.)

1. Seneca Indians — Folklore.   2. Niagara Falls (N.Y. and Ont.) — Folklore.
I. Title.

PS8555.H42242M34 2001   j398.2'089'9755   C2001-930293-2
PZ8.1.C42MA 2001

An adaptation of the Maid of the Mist legend surrounding Niagara Falls, in which a young girl saves her people.

U.S. Publisher Cataloguing-in-Publication Data
(Library of Congress Standards)
Charles, Veronika Martenova

Maiden of the mist : a legend of Niagara Falls / Veronika Martenova Charles
[32}p. : col. ill. ; cm.

Originally published: Toronto: Stoddart, 2001.

Summary: Retelling of a Seneca legend wherein a girl takes destiny into her own hands by going over the falls at Niagara Falls.

ISBN 0-7737-3297-7
ISBN 0-7737-6207-8 (pbk.)

1. Seneca Indians — Folklore — Juvenole literature.   2. Niagara Falls (N.Y. and Ont.) — Folklore — Juvenole literature.
(1. Seneca Indians — Folklore.   2. Niagara Falls (N.Y. and Ont.) — Folklore. I. Title.
398.2 / 089 / 21   E99.S3C47M2 2001

Printed and bound in Hong Kong, China
by Book Art Inc., Toronto

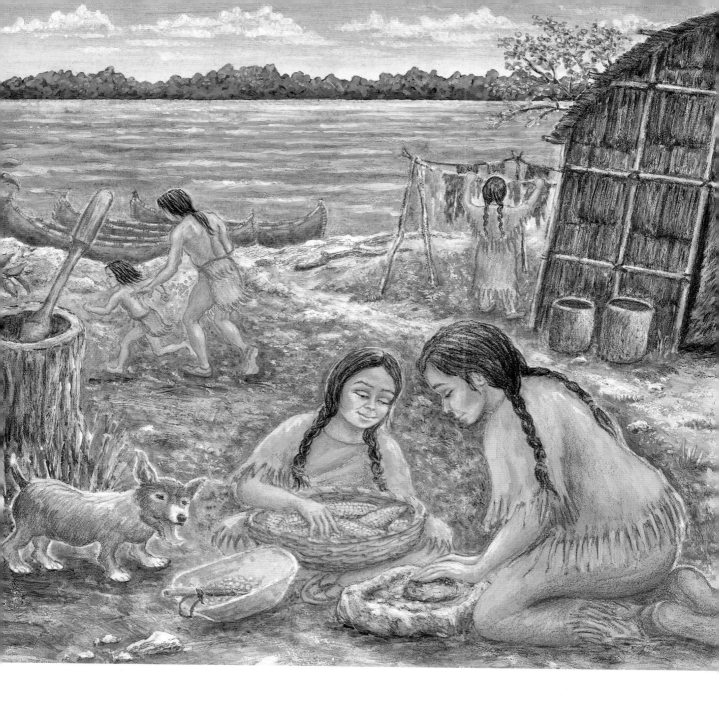

Long ago, a Seneca tribe lived beside the Niagara River, not far upstream from a great waterfall. The river was alive with fish, the fields swelled with corn, and the meadows were covered with sweet berries. For as long as Lelawala could remember, life had been good.

But then one summer sickness came, and many people died. The wife of the chief, Lelawala's mother, was one of them.

The people were worried. "Perhaps the thunder god, Hinu, is angry with us," they said.

Hinu was a mighty being who lived in a cave behind the great falls. He made rain and thunder, but he also protected the people and killed huge underwater snakes that threatened them.

"We must make peace with Hinu," the elders advised. "Perhaps he will lift the curse from us."

So, the people loaded canoes with gifts of food and flowers and sent them down the river, over the falls. Still, day after day, the sickness took young and old alike.

One evening, the medicine man went to the chief. "Hinu is not pleased with our gifts. We must send him something more precious, a thing of youth and beauty."

From the night's shadows, Lelawala listened. She thought of her mother and all the people the sickness had taken. She thought of her desperate father and the fear among those who were left. Lelawala made a decision.

The next morning, Lelawala dressed in her finest clothes and went to her father. "I heard you talking last night. Maybe I can save our people," she said. "I will go down the river to Hinu. I am not afraid."

Her father was stunned. No words came to his lips.

"You must let me go," pleaded Lelawala.

For the last time, she embraced her father. Then she climbed into her canoe. Without another look back, Lelawala set off down the river.

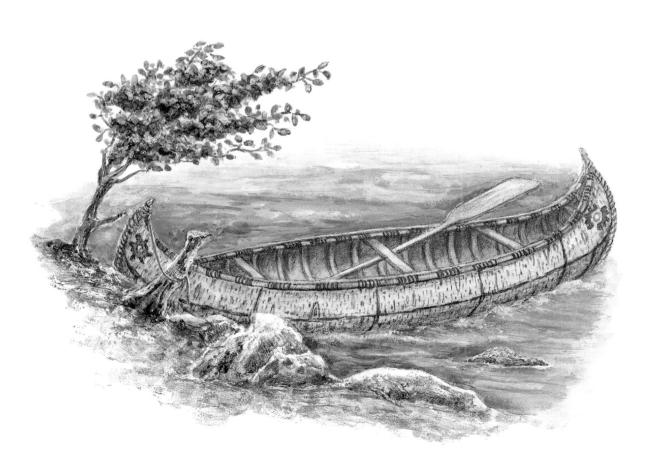

The canoe moved slowly at first, but gained speed as the current grew stronger. In the distance, clouds of smoky mist rose, making the water look like it was on fire. In moments Lelawala would be carried over the falls and swallowed by the river.

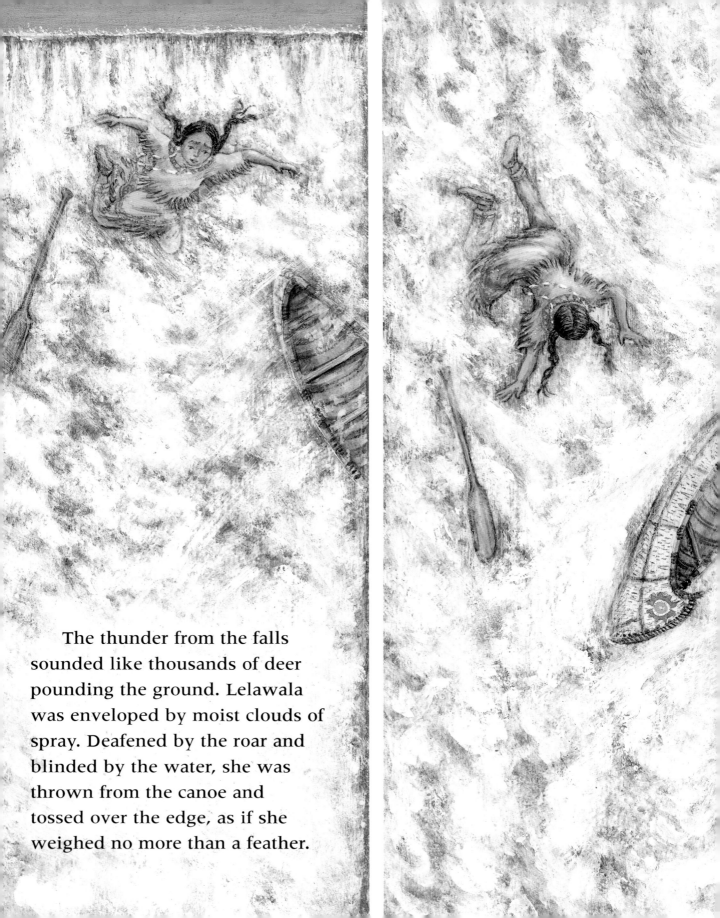

The thunder from the falls
sounded like thousands of deer
pounding the ground. Lelawala
was enveloped by moist clouds of
spray. Deafened by the roar and
blinded by the water, she was
thrown from the canoe and
tossed over the edge, as if she
weighed no more than a feather.

Down,
 down,
  down she fell
   into the boiling
    waters below. Yet there
     was no panic or even fear in her.
     Lelawala felt peaceful and safe,
      almost like she was being
       carried in someone's
        gentle arms.

When the water cleared from Lelawala's eyes, she saw that she was inside a cave. A figure knelt beside her. "I am the son of Hinu," he said. "Stay and take me for your husband."

"I will only stay if you tell me why your father will not help my people," replied Lelawala. "Why is he angry with us?"

"My father is not angry," said the youth. "He is ashamed to let your people know he is not as powerful as they think. There is a monstrous horned snake poisoning the river. That is why your village is dying. The serpent is so enormous, even my father with all of my brothers cannot kill it."

That night, Lelawala thought of her father and appeared in his dream.

"Do not mourn for me, Father," she told him, "for I am safe. Listen, and do as I tell you. I know why our people are sick."

Then she told him about the monstrous snake and how it would appear again.

In two moons' time, the chief and his warriors were waiting by the shore. When the horned serpent rose from the water, they attacked him from their canoes. A fierce battle broke out, and as it did, the sky opened, thunder rolled, and rain poured down.

Bolts of lightning were hurled at the monster. Hinu and his sons had joined the battle. At last, the snake was mortally wounded. The river swept its enormous body toward the falls.

The dying monster got wedged in the boulders at the waterfall's edge. Its head was caught on one side of the river, and its tail on the other. The rocks collapsed under the weight of its writhing body, rearranging the falls into the shape of a bent bow.

That night, the people sang and danced to celebrate the victory. There would be no more sickness. Life, the way they remembered it, could return.

But there were those who were missing from the celebration.

As his people celebrated, the chief slipped away and walked along the riverbank to the falls. There he sat, thinking of those who were gone, and of his daughter in her new life. He listened for her voice in the roar of the water. And he heard it.

Even today, if you happen to stand by Niagara Falls, listen carefully. You just may hear Lelawala and her children calling to each other behind the curtain of water that hides their home.

Author's Note on the Origins of the Legend

Most sacred places on earth have a legend attached to them. The story of *Maiden of the Mist* has been part of Niagara Falls mythology for over 150 years. But there has always been doubt over its origins. Many of today's scholars regard the tale as an invention of guides wanting to enhance the tourist trade.

I was drawn to the story for its fairy tale qualities, and began to search for the legend's roots. I discovered the story is a fusion of two cultures; a European retelling of an Iroquois legend.[1]

In the Iroquois version, a young Seneca girl takes her destiny into her own hands by attempting to escape an unwanted marriage. Her canoe is accidentally swept over the falls, and she is rescued by Hinu, the thunder god. He teaches her how to help rid her people of a disease caused by a monster snake. The story focuses on the conflict between the horned snake and the thunder god. The victory of good over evil results in the creation of Niagara Falls as we know it today.

In the Europeans' version, the focus is on the girl going over the falls.[2] This event reflects the society of the times, in that the girl is portrayed as a passive person who has little control over her own destiny.

In my retelling, I made the story closer to the Iroquois version with its strong heroine. She is not a victim; for her, going over the falls is an act of free will, of courage, and of compassion.

I would like to thank Inge J. Saczkowski, the history librarian for the Niagara Falls Public Library, for helping me in my research and for locating (in the basement vaults) the earliest published accounts. Holding those 150-year-old documents was an emotional high point in the making of this book.

Tom Hill, a Seneca, and the Museum Director of the Woodland Cultural Centre at the Six Nations Reserve in Brantford, Ontario must also be recognized. His input and patient advice about the Iroquois people in earlier times, and his helpful criticism of my paintings for this book have been greatly appreciated.

---

[1] The first recorded accounts of the Iroquois legend were found in: Lewis Henry Morgan, *League of the Ho-dé-no-sau-nee, or Iroquois* (Rochester, New York: Sage & Brother, 1851) 158.

 Another account appeared 32 years later in: Erminnie Adele Platt Smith, *"A Seneca Legend of Hinu and Niagara"* in *Myths of the Iroquois* (Washington, D.C.: Government Printing Office, 1883) 54-55.

[2] The first recorded European version appeared — coincidentally at the same time as the Iroquois version stated above — in: *Burke's Descriptive Guide* (Buffalo, New York: A. Burke, 1850) 101-104.